Underwater Farmyard

For Gilla and Ray – J.S.

For Ella, with love from Mummy

First published in 2002 by Macmillan Children's Books
A division of Pan Macmillan Publishers Limited
20 New Wharf Road, London N1 9RR
Basingstoke and Oxford
Associated companies throughout the world
www.panmacmillan.com

ISBN 0 333 96063 7 HB
ISBN 0 333 96064 5 PB

Text copyright © 2002 Carol Ann Duffy
Illustrations copyright © 2002 Joel Stewart
Moral rights asserted

1 3 5 7 9 8 6 4 2

A CIP catalogue record for this book is available from the British Library.

Printed in Belgium by Proost.

Carol Ann Duffy

Underwater Farmyard

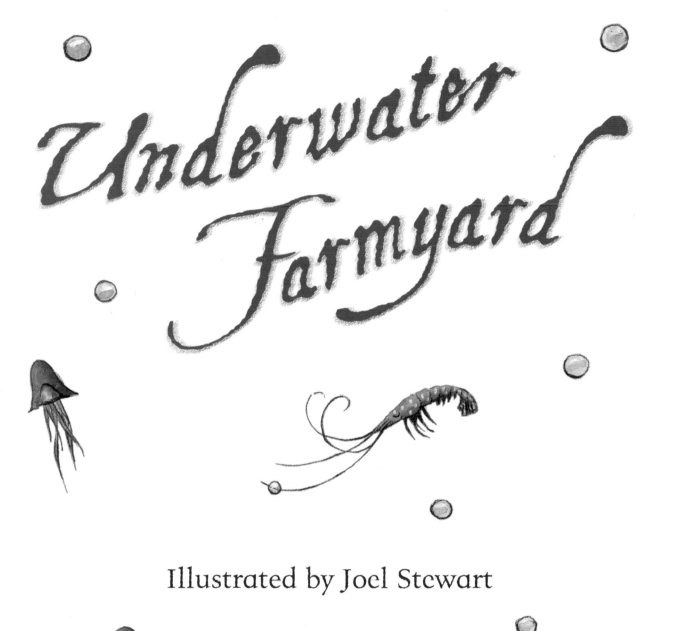

Illustrated by Joel Stewart

MACMILLAN
CHILDREN'S BOOKS

Under the blue-green fields of the Deep

Bleat the bubbly baas of webbed-feet sheep,

Grazing on seaweed,

(Salty, nice)

Swimming up and down in new-washed fleece.

Under the deep wet meadows of the Blue

A herd of sea-cows float and moo,

    Milked by a mermaid

    On a shell milk stool.

The cows are smiling – her hands are cool!

Under the hills and valleys of the Sea

Water pigs snuffle out truffles for tea.

The piglets are playing.

One piglet-girl

Roots in an oyster and winkles out a pearl.

Under the hedges and lanes of the Ocean

Fish-eyed goats are making a commotion.

They're busy nibbling

A shipwrecked boat.

One's guzzling the anchor. (Greedy goat.)

Under the wavy grasses of the Brine

The farm horse is having a whale of a time,

Waltzing with a dolphin

While an octopus swings

With a trumpet and a sax and a violin.

Under the soft black miles of the Drink

Where the last rays of sunset glimmer and sink,

   The underwater farm dog

   Starts to bark:

It's time for sea-bed. It's getting dark.

The lambs in the sheep pen

float and snore.

The sea-cows cuddle up

on freshly soaked straw.

The mermaid reads the calves

a bedtime fable

While the horse and the goat

pillow-fight in the stable.

The piglets snuggle down

in a damp pink huddle

And each pig snuffle

makes a very big bubble.

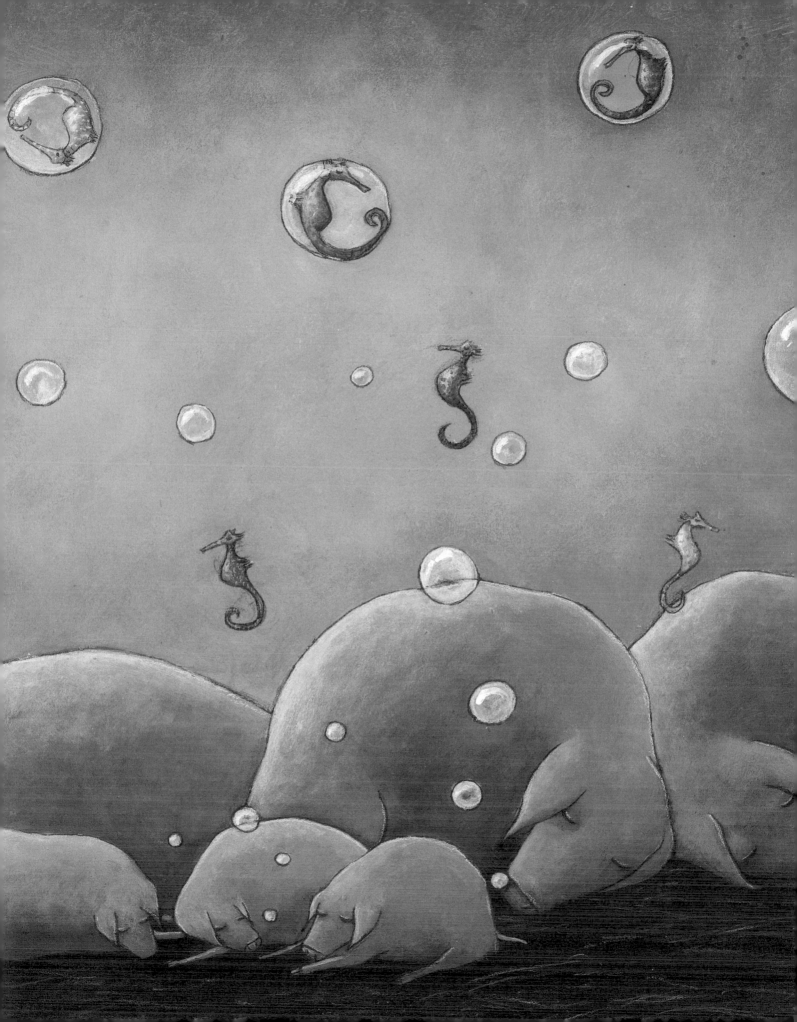

The cockerel yawns.

It's time to settle down,

Hens in the rafters,

dog on the ground.

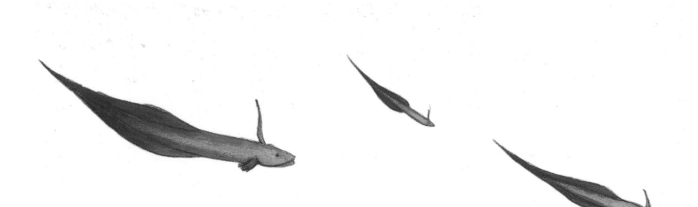

Starfish twinkle in the ocean sky,

Electric eels are comets zooming high.

The moon is the silver of a dolphin's skin

In the watery heaven

Where angelfish swim.

Underwater Farmyard lies safe, lies deep,

As the creatures there fall fast asleep.

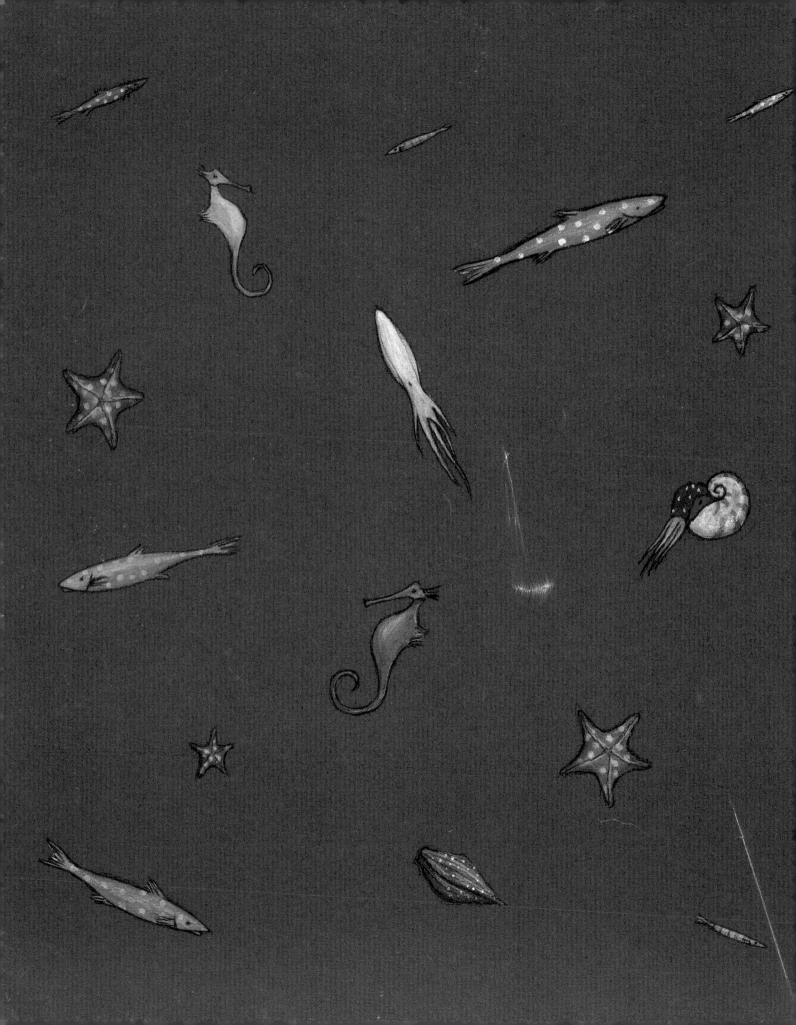